DRACULA

By Bram Stoker

Adapted by Stephanie Spinner

Text illustrations by Jim Spence

STEP-UP CLASSIC CHILLERS™

RANDOM HOUSE 🏠 NEW YORK

Library of Congress Cataloging-in-Publication Data:
Spinner, Stephanie. Dracula. (Step-up classic chillers) SUMMARY:
Having deduced the double identity of Count Dracula, a wealthy
Transylvanian nobleman, a small group of people vow to rid the world of
the evil vampire. [1. Dracula, Count (Fictitious character)—Fiction.
2. Vampires—Fiction. 3. Horror stories] I. Spence, Jim, ill. II. Stoker,
Bram, 1847–1912. Dracula. III. Title. IV. Series. PZ7.S7567Dr 1988
[Fic] 87-23541 ISBN: 0-394-84828-4

Manufactured in the United States of America

16   17   18   19   20

To my father
    —S.S.

Chapter 1

The day was bright and sunny. Birds were singing. Flowers bloomed everywhere. But Jonathan Harker felt sad. The young lawyer had to leave England on business. He knew he would miss his sweetheart, Mina, very much.

Jonathan climbed into the coach.

"Good-bye, my dearest," called Mina. "Hurry back!"

"I will," promised Jonathan. "If all goes well, I will be home in two weeks. And I will write to you every day." The horses broke into a trot. Jonathan was on his way.

By evening he was in London. The next day he crossed the English Channel. Then he took a train to Hungary. After that he went on to Transylvania by horse-drawn coach. There were no trains going there. Transylvania was too small. Too out of the way.

Jonathan looked at the country-side from the coach window. Transylvania was very different from England. The spring air was cold here. The earth was rocky and bare. Tall mountains stood out against the sky. Dark gray clouds hid the late-afternoon sun.

The other people in the coach

wore woollen cloaks and high leather boots. They spoke little. But they seemed friendly. When night fell, they asked Jonathan where he was going.

"Castle Dracula," he answered. Jonathan had been sent by his boss, Mr. Hawkins, to see a man named Count Dracula. The Count had bought a house in London. Jonathan was bringing him the ownership papers. He also carried a letter to the Count from Mr. Hawkins.

Suddenly the passengers looked worried. They spoke together quickly in their own language. A woman with a kind face leaned over and took Jonathan's hand.

"Do not go!" she told him.

Jonathan was surprised. "But—?"

A man said, "It is not good for you to visit Castle Dracula tonight."

"Why not?" asked Jonathan. He saw that the moon was high in the sky. The coach began to go faster.

"Because tonight is the Eve of Saint George," said the man. "All the evil things of the world come out at midnight. You will be in danger."

The other passengers crossed themselves. They began to whisper something. It sounded like a prayer.

"Do not go!" said the woman again.

"But I must!" said Jonathan.

The horses were going even faster now. The coach rocked from side to side. The woman took a cross from around her neck. She pressed it into Jonathan's hand.

TRANSYLVANIA
COACH

"Put it on," she said. As he did, the
coach stopped. They had come to the
Borgo Pass. Someone was supposed
to meet Jonathan there.

The passengers looked out at the

pitch-dark night. They crossed themselves again and again.

Jonathan did not want to show his
fear. He climbed out of the coach.
There was a strange, low rumbling in
the air. The wind howled like a wild
thing. Jonathan could not see anything in the misty blackness. Even
the moon had disappeared. For a
moment he wished that no one
would come to meet him. Then he

could go home. Back to England!

Suddenly the horses reared up on their hind legs. They whinnied. Their eyes rolled.

Out of the dark came a black carriage. It was pulled by four black horses. The driver was a big man wearing a cape. His eyes gleamed red in the light of his lantern.

"Mr. Harker?"

Jonathan nodded. The driver smiled. His teeth were sharp and white. "The Count awaits you," he said.

He called for Jonathan's bags. Someone handed them down from the coach.

The kind woman leaned out the window. She pointed to the cross around Jonathan's neck. She seemed to be telling him to wear it always.

"God save you!" she cried.

Then the coach drove away.

Jonathan climbed into the Count's carriage. He looked at his watch. Midnight. Then he heard a new sound. It was high and sharp, like a long cry. Wolves! The air was cold. But Jonathan began to sweat.

"Don't be a fool!" he told himself. He touched the cross at his neck anyway.

The carriage drove on. Finally it stopped. They had come to a large stone castle. It was so dark and quiet it seemed empty. Jonathan got out. The driver handed down his bags and drove away.

Now there was only the wind and the howling of the wolves. Jonathan shivered. The moon came out. It lit the castle walls with a cold blue glow. Jonathan saw a huge door, carved with demons. Should he knock?

The cry of the wolves grew louder. They were coming closer! Jonathan ran to the door. He banged on it with all his might. Silence. His heart pounded with fear.

Suddenly the door swung open. Standing there was a tall man dressed in black. He was holding a silver lantern. His face was pale. His dark eyes glittered.

"Ah!" he said in a voice that was both deep and eager. "Mr. Harker. Welcome to my house." And he took Jonathan's hand.

Jonathan gasped. The Count's grip was so strong that it hurt. And his hand was colder than ice.

"Please come this way." The Count lifted Jonathan's heavy bags easily. He started down a long stone hallway. At the end of the hallway was a large dining room. A fire burned in the fireplace. Gold dishes filled with food were on the table.

"Please. Eat," said the Count.

"And forgive me for not joining you. I dined earlier."

While Jonathan ate, the Count looked over the ownership papers. Then he read Mr. Hawkins's letter.

"Mr. Hawkins is very fond of you," said the Count. "He writes that you are honest and loyal."

Jonathan was pleased.

"He also writes that you will follow my wishes while you are here," said the Count.

"Of course," answered Jonathan politely.

The Count smiled. In the firelight his teeth looked like fangs. "I know your visit will be an interesting one. But now you must sleep. It is almost dawn."

The Count led Jonathan deep into

the castle. At last they came to a bed-room.

"Rest well," said the Count. "I will see you tomorrow evening."

Moments later Jonathan was sleeping soundly.

Chapter 2

The next day Jonathan ate breakfast by himself. Then he walked through the castle. The halls were empty. Deserted. Did the Count live here all alone?

Jonathan came to a door. It was locked. He tried another door. It was locked too. He tried many more. They were all locked. Strange, thought Jonathan.

Finally he came to a door that opened. Inside was a room full of books. Many were about England. A large map of England was on the wall. It was marked with red circles. There was a circle around London, where the Count's new house was. And there was a circle around Whitby, a town near the sea. Mina visited Whitby every summer. Remembering Mina, Jonathan felt lonely. "I will be home soon," he thought.

Before long it was night. The wolves began to howl. The Count appeared.

"Hello, Mr. Harker," he said. "I see you have found my books about England. I have many. I like England very much."

"Yes," said Jonathan. "So do I."

"Soon I will go there," said the

Count. "To the house I have bought—Carfax Abbey. But first I must learn to speak English."

"You speak English very well!" said Jonathan.

"Not well enough. I wish to speak it perfectly. And you must teach me," said the Count. "Every day, for a month."

Jonathan's face fell. "You want me to stay here for a month?"

The Count's voice was cold. "Yes. And remember, Mr. Hawkins said that you would follow my wishes. Now you must do as I say. Write to him. Tell him you are happy here. That you want to stay with me."

Jonathan was not happy at all. But the Count waited until Jonathan wrote the letter. Then he took it quickly. "I will see you tomorrow," he said. And he was gone.

That night Jonathan could not sleep. He did not want to stay at Castle Dracula. He longed to go home. Why was the Count making him stay? He did not need English lessons. There must be some other reason. But what was it?

The following night the Count came to Jonathan. Again he did not eat. He talked about his family. The Draculas.

"We are strong," he said. "Proud. We have fought many wars. We have won them all. We have killed all our enemies. Nothing can defeat us. Nothing!" The Count's eyes shone. His mouth was cruel. He looked evil.

"I must leave here," thought Jonathan. "This man frightens me."

The next day he was alone again.

He tried to open the castle doors. But
they were locked. He was trapped—a
prisoner!

That night Jonathan was shaving
in his room. He used a small mirror
that he had brought from England.
There were no mirrors in the castle.

He heard someone behind him. It was the Count. But the Count did not appear in Jonathan's mirror. Jonathan turned white. A terrible thought came to him. The Count was not human!

Jonathan's hand began to shake. He cut himself with his razor. A bright line of blood dripped down his face.

The Count stared at Jonathan's cut. "You are bleeding!" he said. His hand reached out for Jonathan's throat.

Jonathan did not dare to move. Then the Count's hand stopped. He drew back. Suddenly he looked sick. "You are wearing a cross!" he gasped.

"Yes," answered Jonathan. He looked in the mirror again. No Count. Was Dracula a ghost?

Now the Count looked angry. "Mirrors cause nothing but trouble!" he said. He grabbed the mirror and threw it out the window. There was a tiny crash as it broke on the ground far below.

The Count gripped Jonathan's arm. His nails were very sharp. They hurt. "I will see you tomorrow, Mr. Harker," he said. It was like a warning.

After the Count had gone, Jonathan stood at his window. Far below, bits of broken mirror sparkled in the moonlight. Jonathan wished that he was on the ground too. Out-

side Castle Dracula. On his way
home.

He leaned out the window. It was
a long, long way down.

Chapter 3

The next day Jonathan went to the library room. He began to write in his diary. He used a special code. He did not want the Count to understand what he wrote.

"I am afraid," wrote Jonathan. "Afraid that I am going crazy. I cannot believe my eyes anymore. Last night I was standing at my window. It was very late. A dark shape came down the castle wall. At first I could not tell what it was. Then I saw. It was the Count. He was crawling down the castle. Head first! Like a giant spider! He crawled all the way down to the ground. And then he disappeared.

"Did I really see this? Or am I losing my mind?"

Jonathan closed his diary. He felt scared. Mixed up. "This is like a bad dream," he thought. He put his head down on the table and cried. Then he fell asleep.

The library grew dark. Jonathan woke. He was so tired and sleepy that he could not move. He heard a whisper—a woman's voice. Then he heard another woman answering. And then a third.

"Let me have him," said one voice.

"No. It is my turn," said another.

Jonathan saw three women coming toward him. Their faces were
white. Their eyes were red.

"He has enough blood for all of
us," said the third woman. She
leaned over Jonathan. He wanted to
push her away. But somehow he
could not.

"I will go first," she said. She
licked her lips. Then Jonathan felt
her sharp teeth on his neck.

Suddenly he heard an angry shout.
It was the Count.

"Leave him!" cried the Count.
"He belongs to me! I have told you.
This man is mine!"

The women backed away. "But what about us?" they asked. "Are we to have nothing?"

"You can have him tomorrow. When I am finished with him," said the Count. "Now—leave!"

Jonathan heard the Count's words and blacked out. When he woke, it was morning. He was in his bed.

Jonathan sat up. He remembered the three women and the Count. And he knew he had to get out of Castle Dracula right away. Or he would be a dead man.

Jonathan left his room. He began searching for a way out of the castle. He moved quickly. He knew the Count would be back that night.

First Jonathan tried all the doors. Then he went up and down the hallways. No luck. He turned a new corner and saw some steps. Could this be the way out?

Jonathan climbed down and down. He came to a room deep under the ground. The air was cold and damp. Bats flew above him in the dark.

He lit a candle. The room was full of long wooden boxes. Were they coffins for dead people? Then Jonathan saw that the boxes had earth in them. The earth was from the floor of the room. He looked at the boxes more closely. Each one had a label.

TO: COUNT DRACULA

CARFAX ABBEY

LONDON, ENGLAND

Then Jonathan saw four of the boxes in a row. He looked inside. There were the three women—each one in a box! Their eyes were open. But they did not move when Jonathan came near.

"Are they asleep?" he wondered. "Or dead?"

Jonathan came to the fourth box. Inside lay the Count. His eyes were open. There was blood on his lips.

"Ugh!" Jonathan drew back. He began to think, hard.

The Count had bought a house in London. Carfax Abbey. He was going to send boxes there. Boxes just like the one he was resting in. Would these boxes hold creatures like the Count? Like the three women? Evil creatures that drank blood?

"No!" screamed Jonathan. "I will not let it happen!" He picked up a shovel. He raised it high over his head. He hit the Count as hard as he could. But Dracula only smiled.

Jonathan dropped the shovel and ran. Up the winding steps. Back to his room. To the open window. It was the only way out.

"If I fall, I will die," he thought. "But even death is better than being Dracula's prisoner!"

Jonathan crawled out the window. He hung on to the ledge. He felt for a place to rest his foot. A stone. A crack. Anything. Then he found a crack. And another.

Inch by inch, Jonathan climbed down the castle wall. Slowly, and with great care. For now there was

only one thing on his mind. He had
to get back to England. Somehow,
Dracula had to be stopped!

Chapter 4

Mina and her friend Lucy were walking near the ocean. It was June. They had just come to Whitby for a holiday.

Lucy was smiling. "I have so much to tell you!" she said to Mina.

Mina tried to smile back. She couldn't. Her face was troubled.

"Mina! What's the matter? Is something wrong?"

"Yes," said Mina. "I am worried about Jonathan. He left England many weeks ago. At first he wrote to me every day. About his trip. About Transylvania. Then, suddenly, the letters stopped. I don't know why."

"Maybe he's on his way home," said Lucy.

"But he would write to me. To tell me," said Mina. "I'm afraid. I can't help it. I think he's in danger."

Lucy frowned. Then she had an idea. "Maybe Arthur can help," she said. Arthur was Lucy's boyfriend. "Arthur has friends in Hungary. They can check with hospitals. With the police. Don't worry, Mina. We will find Jonathan!"

Mina smiled. "That is a good idea, Lucy. I feel much better now."

The girls walked on, arm in arm. Then the sky began to darken.

"It looks like rain," said Lucy. "We had better go back to the house."

When they got home, they found Dr. John Seward there. He was visiting Lucy's mother, Mrs. Westenra.

Lucy was glad to see John Seward. He was a good doctor. He was also a good friend.

"John!" she said. "How is my mother?"

"She is a little better," said Dr. Seward. "But her heart is weak. She needs rest. Quiet. Some good sea air. Let's hope the weather won't be like this for long!"

Outside the sky was almost black.

Hours later, a storm was in full force. Wind and rain beat at the house. Lightning split the sky.

Mina and Lucy looked out their

bedroom window. When the lightning flashed, they could see the ocean.

"What a terrible storm," said Lucy. "I hope it doesn't keep Mother awake." Then she saw something on the water.

"Mina, look! Down at the harbor!"

The girls saw a big ship. It was tossing back and forth on the stormy sea.

"It will crash on the rocks," said Lucy.

"We must pray for the men on board," said Mina. The girls said a prayer together. Then they went to sleep.

The next day was sunny. The girls were eating lunch when Mrs. Westenra joined them.

"My maid told me something strange," she said. "About a ship that washed up on the beach."

"That must be the ship we saw last night," said Mina. "We were afraid it would sink. Is the crew all right?"

"That is what is strange," said Mrs. Westenra. "The ship had no crew. It carried only boxes. Fifty long, narrow boxes, like coffins— filled with earth."

Mina and Lucy looked at each other. They did not know what to think.

"I heard something else," said Mrs. Westenra. "There was a big dog on the ship. Almost like a wolf. My maid said it killed someone and ran away. No one could find it!" Mrs. Westenra looked pale. "It makes me sick just to think of it," she said.

"Mother," said Lucy. "Please stay calm. You know what Dr. Seward says. You must rest. You must not worry!"

"That is not all I am worried about," said Mrs. Westenra. "You are walking in your sleep again, Lucy. I am afraid you will hurt yourself."

"I won't," said Lucy. "Mina will

watch over me. Won't you, Mina?"

"Like a hawk," Mina promised.

Later that day Mrs. Westenra talked to Mina alone. "Please lock your bedroom door tonight," she said. "Then Lucy won't be able to get out. She will be safe."

Mina agreed. But late that night she woke up to find Lucy gone. Her bed was empty. And the bedroom door was open.

Mina jumped out of bed. She put on a cape and found one of Lucy's shawls. "I will wrap her in this when I find her," she thought. Then she left the house.

Outside the wind was blowing. Clouds flew across the moon. It was dark one minute, bright the next. Mina was not sure which way to go.

She couldn't call Lucy's name. Mrs. Westenra might wake up. So she set off for East Cliff. She and Lucy liked to sit there and watch the ships. Maybe Lucy had gone there in her sleep.

Mina started running. Up the hill. Past the big church. Past the quiet graveyard. Soon she could see East Cliff. She strained her eyes. Was that Lucy in her white nightgown?

"Lucy! Lucy!" she called. Then she saw something long and dark. It was bending over her friend. At the sound of Mina's voice, the dark figure looked up.

Mina saw a white face and red, gleaming eyes. A cloud passed over the moon. When the moon came out again, Lucy was alone. Mina ran to

her. She was still asleep. Her breath came in long gasps.

Mina wrapped the shawl around Lucy. She pinned it at Lucy's neck with a big pin. Then she woke her friend gently and led her home.

"Mina," said Lucy in a sleepy voice, "my mother will worry. Please don't tell her about this."

"I won't," said Mina. She unpinned Lucy's shawl. Then she tucked her into bed.

"Thank you," said Lucy. She turned to go to sleep. Mina saw two red marks on Lucy's neck. They were like pin pricks.

"How did they get there?" Mina wondered. "Did I scratch Lucy with the shawl pin?" The question was still on her mind as she fell asleep.

Chapter 5

Three days later Lucy was pale and weak. The marks on her neck had not healed.

Mina was worried. "What is wrong with her?" she asked Dr. Seward.

"I don't know," he said. "It puzzles me. But my old friend Van Helsing is coming. He is a very good doctor. He knows about many, many different kinds of sicknesses. Maybe he can tell us what is wrong with Lucy."

"I hope so," said Mina. "I will

think about her every day while I am away."

Mina was going to meet Jonathan. He was in a hospital in Hungary. His letter said that he had been there for many weeks. At first he had not known who he was. Or where he was. Then, slowly, he had gotten better. Now he was well enough to travel. Mina could bring him back to England.

A few days after Mina left, Van Helsing came to see Lucy.

"Hello, my dear. How are you feeling?" he asked.

Lucy tried to sit up. She was very weak. "I am so tired," she said.

"Rest, rest," said Van Helsing. He sat down and took Lucy's hand. "When did you first feel this way?"

"Last week," said Lucy. "Right after . . ."

"After what?" asked Van Helsing.

"Right after my dream."

"Tell me about it," said Van Helsing.

"I dreamed that something called me out of bed. To East Cliff. And when it called, I followed. I had to."

"What was it?" asked Van Helsing.

"It was long. Dark. It had red eyes. And its teeth were white. . . ." Lucy's hand went to her throat. Her eyes closed. "Such a strange dream," she said. Then she slept.

Van Helsing saw the marks on Lucy's throat. "Oh no!" he whispered. "Can it be true?" He rushed

out of the room and found Dr.
Seward.

"I must go home," he said. "I think
I know what is wrong with Lucy. But
I must look at my books to be sure.
Until I come back, stay in Lucy's

room at night. She must not be alone after dark!"

That night Dr. Seward sat in Lucy's bedroom. He tried to stay awake. But he couldn't. Before long his eyes closed.

Soon after he fell asleep, a big bat came to the window. Its wings knocked at the glass. It wanted to come in. Lucy woke. When she saw the bat, she got up. She opened the window.

The bat flew into the room. Then it changed—into Dracula.

"You are mine," he said to Lucy.

"Yes," she answered.

Dracula bit Lucy's neck. He drank her blood. Then he turned into a bat again and flew away.

The next morning Dr. Seward

woke up and looked at Lucy. She was almost dead.

He sent a telegram to Van Helsing. It said, "Come at once. Lucy is much worse."

Van Helsing returned and looked at Lucy's still, white body. "She needs blood," he said. "Right away!"

Arthur, Lucy's boyfriend, came to help. "I will give her all the blood she needs," he said.

"Thank you, Arthur," said Van Helsing. "It may save her life." Van Helsing quickly took blood from Arthur. Then he injected the blood into Lucy's arm.

After a while Lucy's cheeks turned pink. She moved. Then she opened her eyes. "Arthur!" she said. "When did you come?"

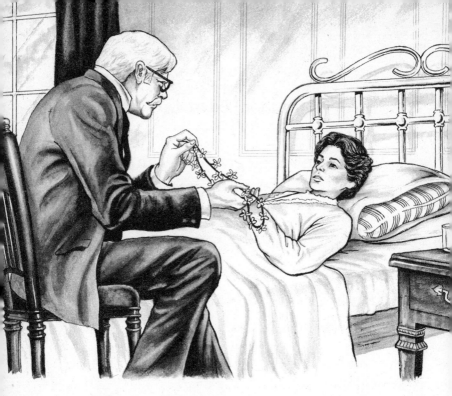

"This morning," said Arthur. "When I heard how sick you were."

"Arthur has helped to keep you alive," said Van Helsing. "Now we must do a few more things to help you." He opened his bag. "You must wear these flowers around your neck. I will hang more of them over your door."

"Garlic flowers," said Lucy. "What good will they do?"

"They will protect you," said Van Helsing. "Keep them around your neck. It is important. And do not open the window. Promise me."

"I promise," said Lucy.

Late that night Lucy heard a high, sharp cry outside her window. A minute later her bedroom door opened. Her mother came in.

"I heard a strange sound," said Mrs. Westenra. "Are you all right, Lucy?"

"Yes, Mother," said Lucy. "You will get cold standing there. Come and lie in bed with me."

Mrs. Westenra lay down beside Lucy. She saw the garlic flowers around Lucy's neck. "Why are you wearing these silly things?" she asked. She pulled them off.

"Dr. Van Helsing said I must keep them on—"

There was a loud crash at the window. A big wolf broke through the glass. It showed its teeth with a growl. Mrs. Westenra screamed. She fell back on the bed, suddenly still.

"Mother!" cried Lucy. Mrs. Westenra did not answer. She was dead.

Then the wolf at the window changed—into Dracula.

"Come," he said. "Come to me."

Lucy had to obey. She went to the Count. He drank her blood. And then he was gone.

The next morning Van Helsing and Arthur stood over Lucy's bed. "I cannot believe it," said Arthur. "Mrs.

Westenra dead. Lucy dying. It is terrible."

"Yes," said Van Helsing. "It IS terrible. Mrs. Westenra's heart was weak. She died of fright. And Lucy is being killed—by something that is not human. By a vampire!"

"What!" said Arthur. "Do you mean to say that vampires are real? I thought they were only in stories."

"They are real," said Van Helsing. "And they are very dangerous."

Suddenly Lucy's eyes flew open. She saw Arthur, and a smile came over her white face. Now she had fangs instead of teeth.

"Arthur," she called. Her voice was low and hungry. "Come to me. Kiss me!"

Van Helsing held Arthur back. "It is not safe to touch her," he said. "She is no longer human."

Arthur did not want to believe it. He ran to Lucy. But she fell back, dead. Slowly, the red marks on her throat went away. A look of peace came over her face.

"She can rest now," said Arthur. "It is over."

"No," said Van Helsing. "It is only the beginning."

"What do you mean?" asked Arthur.

"We must drive a stake through her heart," said Van Helsing. "Or she will rise from her grave."

"No!" cried Arthur. "I will not allow it!"

"My friend, you must change your mind," said Van Helsing. "Or Lucy will walk the earth forever. As a vampire!"

Chapter 6

Mina and Jonathan walked arm in arm down a busy street in London. They had been married. Now they were on their way to their new house.

The sky was getting dark. The street was crowded. Suddenly Jonathan stopped. He held tight to Mina's arm.

"Jonathan, what is it?" asked Mina. "You're shaking!"

Jonathan stared at a tall man with

dark eyes who was passing. "Can he be here, in London?" gasped Jonathan. "Then the nightmare has come true!"

Mina made Jonathan sit down. "Who was that man?" she asked. "Do you know him?"

Jonathan was silent for a long time. Then he said, "I never told you what happened to me in Transylvania. I saw strange things there. Awful things. Sometimes I thought I was going crazy. Or dreaming it all. So I kept a diary. I wrote down what I saw at Castle Dracula.

"Now HE is here. And I must find out. Did I dream it? Or is Dracula really a monster?

"Will you read my diary, Mina? And tell me what you think?"

"Of course I will read it," said Mina. Then she led Jonathan home.

A telegram was on the doorstep. "My friends," it said, "there is terrible news. Mrs. Westenra died two days ago. Lucy died yesterday. The causes of their deaths are not clear. Signed, in great sadness, John Seward."

Mina and Jonathan were shocked. "How did our friends die?" they wondered. They decided to see Dr. Seward. Maybe he could tell them more.

Van Helsing and Arthur stood at Lucy's grave. It was nighttime. Van Helsing wanted to prove that Lucy was a vampire. When he opened the grave, it was empty.

"But—where is her body?" asked
Arthur.

"She has gone to look for a vic-
tim," said Van Helsing. "So she can
drink blood. We must find her, and
stop her."

They began looking for Lucy near the graveyard. Before long they found a little boy. He was standing quietly in the dark, near a tree.

"What are you doing here?" asked Van Helsing. "You are too young to be out so late. You should be at home. In bed."

"The beautiful lady told me to wait here," answered the little boy.

"The beautiful lady?" asked Van Helsing. "Who is she?" Then he saw two small bites on the boy's neck. "Oh no!" he said to Arthur. "Lucy has begun!"

The men took the little boy home. Then they returned to the tree.

"Lucy will come back here for the child," Van Helsing said. "We will wait for her."

A long time passed. Then they heard a woman's voice. "Come. Come to me," the voice called.

Lucy appeared. But she did not look like she used to. Now her mouth was stained with blood. Her teeth were fangs. She was a vampire!

Lucy saw Arthur and reached out for him. "My love!" she cried. "Come to me!"

Van Helsing held a cross up to Lucy. When she saw it, she made a sound like a growl. Her eyes glowed red with fear. She ran away.

Arthur wept. "You were right," he said to Van Helsing. "She is not Lucy anymore. She is—evil!"

Van Helsing answered softly, "I am sorry. I know you loved her." He looked at the sky. "Dawn is coming.

Soon Lucy must return to her grave. When she does, we will drive a stake through her heart. Then her life as a vampire will be over. And she will rest. Forever."

The two men sat down to wait.

The next day, Van Helsing called Dr. Seward, Arthur, Mina, and Jonathan together. They met at Dr. Seward's house in London. When Jonathan came in, he said, "I have just learned that we are all in danger!"

"What do you mean?" asked Dr. Seward.

"It is Dracula," said Jonathan. "When I was at his castle, I saw many strange things. I thought I might be dreaming. Or crazy. But now I know what happened there was real. That Dracula is real. And he is here in London. Worse yet, the house he bought—Carfax Abbey—is right next door!"

"So close!" gasped Dr. Seward.

Van Helsing stood. "Friends," he said, "we face a strong enemy. Dracula almost killed Jonathan. He scared Lucy's mother to death. He turned Lucy into a vampire. Now he is here in London. He will strike again, and again. His victims will become vampires—like poor Lucy."

Mina shivered. "Why is he so evil?" she asked.

"Long ago," said Van Helsing, "Dracula was a great soldier. He won many battles. Then he began to lose. He could not stand it. So he made a

pact with the Devil. He gave up his
soul—for victory.

"Now he is doomed to live forever.
He feeds on the blood of humans. No
one is safe from him."

"He must be stopped," said Dr.
Seward. "But how? He has magic
powers."

"It will not be easy," said Van
Helsing. "Dracula is as strong as

twenty men. He can order clouds and fog to hide him. He can force his victims to obey—by staring at them. He can change his shape. He can turn himself into a wolf, or a bat."

"We will never beat him," said Arthur. "He is too smart. Too strong."

"No," said Van Helsing. "A cross can stop him. So can garlic. Or holy water. He can only change his shape at night. During the day his powers leave him and he must rest. He must lie in a coffin filled with earth from Transylvania."

"Those boxes on the empty boat at Whitby!" said Mina. "Were they Dracula's?"

"Yes," said Jonathan. "They were the boxes I saw at Castle Dracula. He was sending them to London. To his house—Carfax Abbey."

Van Helsing stood up. "We must go to Carfax Abbey," he said. "We will destroy the boxes. Then Dracula will have no place to rest. He will grow weak. And we can win our battle against him!"

The group joined hands. "Does everyone swear to fight against Dracula? And to destroy him?" asked Van Helsing.

"Yes!" said Dr. Seward.

"Yes!" said Arthur.

"Yes!" said Jonathan and Mina.

"Good," said Van Helsing. "Now we can begin."

Chapter 7

Van Helsing led the way. Jonathan, Arthur, and Dr. Seward followed. They were in Carfax Abbey, looking for Dracula's boxes.

The men hurried through the big old house. They had to work in the day while Dracula slept. He could not harm them while the sun was in the sky.

The men climbed downstairs to a room underground. The farther down they went, the worse it smelled.

The smell was of things dead and dying. It made them choke.

"His spirit is near," said Van Helsing. "The boxes must be very close."

The men held their lanterns high. The floor of the underground room was covered with boxes. Twenty-nine of them.

"There should be fifty," said Jonathan. "Where are the other twenty-one?"

"Dracula is clever," said Van Helsing. "He has hidden them in more than one place. We must split up and search everywhere. The docks. The railroad stations. We must find those other boxes. But first let us destroy these."

While the men were away, Mina

was at home alone. At ten o'clock she went to bed. Before long she heard a quiet, hissing sound.

At first she could see nothing in the dark. Then a cold, misty cloud crept over to her bed. It changed its shape—into something long and dark. Something with a white face and wild red eyes.

Mina could not tell if she was dreaming. She felt too heavy to speak. Too heavy to move. The red eyes came closer and closer. Then everything turned black.

When Jonathan came home, Mina was sound asleep. She slept very late the next day. When she woke, she was tired and weak. She felt like crying. But she did not know why.

Jonathan did not see that anything

was wrong. Not that day or the next. He and the others were working hard to find the missing boxes. So hard that they did not notice what was happening to Mina.

Dracula was drinking Mina's blood. Every night he came to her in a cloud. Every day she got weaker. She grew afraid of her strange, dark dreams. But by day it was hard to remember them.

Then one day Arthur came to Van Helsing with good news. "I have found out where the missing boxes are," he said. "An old man who works at the railroad station told me. All the boxes came from Whitby on a train. Then some were sent to Carfax Abbey. Others went to the south of London, and to the east. Still others were sent to a house in the center of town. In Piccadilly. I have all the addresses!"

Van Helsing packed his bag with crosses, garlic, and holy water. "We must get Arthur and Jonathan," he said. "We have work to do!"

They hurried to Jonathan's house. There they were met with a terrible sight. Mina was crying as if she could never stop. There was blood on her nightgown. Blood on her face. And there were two bright red marks on her neck.

Jonathan could hardly speak. His eyes burned with anger. "He has been here!" he said at last. "That monster—Dracula. He has been feeding on Mina's blood!"

"He told me he would kill Jonathan if I made a sound," cried Mina. "And after he drank my blood, he—" She had trouble saying it.

"What, my dear?" asked Van Helsing.

"He cut his chest. He made me drink HIS blood. 'Now you are in my power,' he said. 'You will come when I call. You will help me fight my enemies!' "

Mina cried harder than ever. "I would rather die than help him! What shall I do?"

"Wait here," said Van Helsing. "Try to rest. If our work goes well, you will have nothing to fear."

Jonathan took Mina back to her

room. After a while he joined his friends.

"We must hurry," said Van Helsing. "Before Dracula's power over Mina grows any stronger. We have destroyed the twenty-nine boxes at Carfax. Now we must find the others. Arthur, you and Seward will work together. Destroy the boxes in the south of London. Jonathan and I will take care of the boxes in the east. Then let us all meet at the house in Piccadilly."

The men hurried off. Hours later they were together again in Piccadilly. Arthur and Seward had destroyed nine boxes. Jonathan and Van Helsing had destroyed eleven.

Now Jonathan was adding numbers in his head. Carfax—twenty-nine. South and east London—twelve. Piccadilly—eight. All together, they had found forty-nine boxes. One was still missing!

Chapter 8

The men went back to Jonathan's house. They talked about what they should do.

"We must find that last box," said Jonathan.

Mina started to leave the room. "Do not talk about your plans around me," she said. "It is not safe. I am in Dracula's power. He can look into my mind. If I know your plans, he will find them out."

"Wait," said Van Helsing. "You

say Dracula can see into your mind. What if it works two ways? What if you can look into HIS mind? You may be the key to finding him."

Van Helsing asked Mina to sit down. "I am going to hypnotize you," he said. "It is our last hope."

Mina agreed. Before long she was in a trance. Then Van Helsing began to ask her questions.

"Where are you?"

Mina spoke slowly. "I feel waves. I am on the ocean. I am in a wooden box. On a ship. Soon I will be home. Far from my enemies. Safe . . ."

Van Helsing woke Mina. "It worked!" he said. "Dracula is on a ship. He is running away. To the only safe place left to him—Castle Dracula."

Now everyone knew what had to be done. They had to catch Dracula before he reached his castle.

Early the next day they set off for Transylvania. Van Helsing knew of a shortcut. They prayed it would get them there before the Count.

But the trip took longer than they hoped. Bad luck slowed them down. Or was Dracula reading Mina's mind? Did he cause them to miss a train? To lose a wheel from their coach? They would never know.

At last the group reached Transylvania. They stopped to rest outside a tall forest. The sun was setting. High on a hill, a stone castle stood against the red sky.

Jonathan shivered. "Castle Dracula!" he said.

The sky turned black. The air grew cold. A foggy mist crept down the hill toward the group.

"He is near," said Van Helsing. "At night, in this place, his power is very strong."

Van Helsing took crosses and holy

water from his bag. He sprinkled the water in a big circle around the group.

"Stay inside the circle," he said to everyone. "It will protect us."

The foggy mist came closer. Three women with wild red eyes appeared. They floated close to Mina.

"Sister," they called. "Join us."

Mina got up. "I must obey," she whispered. She walked to the edge of the circle. Then she stopped. She could not step over the holy water!

Van Helsing put his arm around Mina. He held a cross up to the three vampires. "Go!" he cried. "Go away, you devils!"

The vampires hissed. Their red eyes flashed. They backed away.

The group stayed awake all night.

The vampires came close. But they
could not break into the circle. So
Mina was safe.

At last the dawn came. The vampires disappeared. Van Helsing and Seward went to the castle. They found the three vampires resting in their boxes.

"Rest now," said Van Helsing. "Your nights of searching for victims are over." Then he drove stakes into their hearts.

Now the group had one thing left to do. They had to wait—for Dracula. They hid near the road to the castle. Hours went by. Still he did not come. Then, just as the sun began to set . . .

"Look!" said Jonathan. "A wagon. With a coffin on it!"

Arthur and Jonathan ran in front of the wagon. "Stop!" they shouted.

The men in the wagon looked

mean. They jumped down and started to fight. Arthur and Jonathan drew their guns. The men gave up and ran away.

"Open the box!" cried Van Helsing. "Hurry! When the sun sets, he will have his powers back!"

Dracula lay still in the open box. But his eyes flashed. He stared at Van Helsing as if to stop him.

Van Helsing would not be stopped. He raised his wooden stake high. Then he drove it straight into Dracula's heart. Arthur and Jonathan helped to drive it in.

"For Lucy!" cried Arthur.

"For Mina!" cried Jonathan.

Dracula's red eyes closed. Then he crumbled slowly into dust. A roaring wind rushed out of the coffin. When

it died away, Dracula was gone.

Mina's hand went to her throat. "His power has truly ended," she said. "Look." The red marks on her throat were gone. She was herself again.

Dr. Seward, Arthur, Van Helsing, Mina, and Jonathan joined hands. By the light of the setting sun, they said a prayer of thanks together.

STEPHANIE SPINNER likes old castles and dark, foggy nights. But she has never bitten anyone's neck, and her eyes do not turn red when she is angry. Ms. Spinner lives in New York City and works as an editor of children's books.

JIM SPENCE and his wife live in Bohemia, Long Island, which is nowhere near Transylvania. He is a young artist who devotes full time to illustration. His work has appeared not only in books, but in magazines and galleries as well. *Dracula* is Mr. Spence's first book for Random House.